A Note to Parents & Caregivers—

Reading Stars books are designed to build confidence in the earliest of readers. Relying on word repetition and visual cues, each book features fewer than 50 words.

You can help your child develop a lifetime love of reading right from the very start. Here are some ways to help your beginning reader get going:

 Read the book aloud as a first introduction

 Run your fingers below the words as you read each line

 Give your child the chance to finish the sentences or read repeating words while you read the rest.

⭐ Encourage your child to read aloud every day!

Every Child can be a Reading Star!

Published in the United States by Xist Publishing
www.xistpublishing.com

First Edition
eISBN: 978-1-5324-1597-5
Paperback ISBN: 978-1-5324-1598-2
Hardcover ISBN: 978-1-5324-1599-9
Printed in the United States of America

Inside Birds

Cecilia Smith
Jenna Palm

xist Publishing

Bird in a store.

9

Bird in a restaurant.

13

Bird in a party.

and when they do,

23

and they will thank you.

I am a Reading Star
because I can read the
words in this book:

a
and
bird
birds
do
go
help
house
in
inside
just
on
out
party

plane
pool
restaurant
school
sometimes
store
thank
them
they
train
when
will
you

xist Publishing